MY DEAR LIFE SAYINGS

SRI RAM.K

Copyright © Sri Ram.k
All Rights Reserved.

I WOULD LIKE TO DEDICATE

THIS BOOK TO MYSELF

Contents

Foreword

THIS BOOK IS CONSISTS OF MANY PEOPLE
LIFE STRUGGLE IN THEIR DAY TO DAY LIFE
SOME PEOPLE WILL TRY TO EXPRESS THEIR
PAIN TO OTHERS AND SOME PEOPLE WILL
STORE THEIR PAIN IN THEMSELVES
THIS BOOK WILL HELP THEM TO KNOW.
THE REALITY OF PEOPLE AND MAKES
THEM MOVE ON THEIR LIFE

Preface

THIS BOOK IS INSPIRED
BY MY LIFE
EVERY PERSON JUNCTURE
PROBLEMS IN DAY TO DAY LIFE
THEY WON'T EXPRESS THEIR PAIN
AND EMOTIONS TO OTHERS BUT BY
READING QUOTES THEY GET BE AMBITIOUS
THEY WILL EXPRESS THEIR INTENSION
AND SMILE IN THEIR FACES

Acknowledgements

I WOULD LIKE TO SAY
"THANKS YOU
" TO MY FATHER
MR. RAMA CHANDRA MURTHY
TO MY MOTHER
MRS. NAGA SRIDEVI
TO MY AUNTY
SARDA ALURI
TO MY INSPIRATION
JEEVITA GOWD
THANKING MY AUNTY AND JEEVITA
TO STANDS BESIDE ME AND
WHEN I'M IN THE DARK WORLD
THEY MOTIVATED AND STAND
BESIDES ME GAVE A ME RE BIRTH
AND MADE ME STRONG
THIS NOVEL IS PURELY WRITTEN WITH
NEAT INTENTIONS NOT TO HURT
ANY PEOPLE .

Prologue

THIS BOOK OF QUOTES HELPS
US TO REALIZE FROM THE
HURTING PAST AND KEEPS
THE PEOPLE TO GET MOTIVATED
AND START THEIR INDIVIDUAL
GROWTH MAKE OTHERS TO
CRY BY WATCHING THEIR SUCCESS.
PUTTING BACK STEP IS NOT
THE KEY TO SUCCESS
ACCEPT THE BETRAYAL AND TRY
TO SHOW YOUR SUCCESS WITH YOUR SMILE

Author Pick

CONTACT ME ON - SRI_RAM_K__

Author Bio

I STARTED TRAVELLING THE WORLD
TO EXPLORE IT IN DETAILED MANNER
TO SEE AND OBSERVE THE DIFFERENCE
BETWEEN EVERY INDIVIDUALS AND
THEIR ATTITUDE AND BEHAVIOUR.
I HAVE OBSERVED MANY DIFFERENT KIND
OF CUSTOMS AND MINDSETS OF PEOPLE
ACCORDING TO THEIR REGION
I OBSERVED HOW PEOPLE WILL CHANGE
THEIR ROLLS IN ACCORDING TO THE
TOUGH SITUATIONS.
I WAS SEARCHING TO UNDERSTAND
DIFFERENT MINDSETS OF PEOPLE
AND HOW THEY TREAT ACCORDING
TO THEIR NEEDS .
I WAS INTRESTED IN WRITING FOR
A LONG TIME .
WITH VARIOUS TRANINGS AND
UNDERSTANDING
I STARTED WORKING ON THIS .
BECAUSE WE CAN EXPRESS OUR EMOTIONS
AND PAINS IN OUR BOOK AND CAN GIVE
MEANINGFULL QUOTES TO THE PEOPLE
FOR MANY PROBLEMS THEIR WILL BE NO
SOLUTION BY ANYONE BUT THESE NOVELS
GIVES IDEAS AND MOTIVATION TO OVERCOME
FROM THE TOUGH TIME

DEAR LIFE SAYINGS

WHEN EVERYONE LEAVE HAND.
THERE IS A HOPE IN THE HANDS
OF HOPE IN THE HANDS OF LORD
WHO CATCH US WHEN WE ARE
ABOUT TO FALL

NEVER MEANS NEVER SHARE YOUR
FEELINGS TO ANYONE OR UPLOAD
IN SOCIAL MEDIA BECAUSE YOU
NEVER KNEW WHO IS DYING TO
SEE YOU IN THE PAIN .

YOU DOESN'T HAVE THE RIGHT
TO SAY LOVE YOU UNTIL YOU
CAN LOVE YOURSELF.
WHEN NO ONE STAND
BESIDE US.

IMPOSIBLLE THING ALWAYS
DOESNT BE TRUE ALWAYS .
SOMETIMES IT COMES WITH
OUR VIEWS AND PRESCRIPTION.

SOMETIMES ITS REALLY IMPORTANT
TO FEEL BETRAYAL IN LIFE.
SOMETIMES UNIVERSE GIVES
THE PAIN WHICH WE COULDN'T
BEAR SO ONE DAY .

WE COULD COME UP WITH
THE BEST VERSION OF
OURSELVES.

WHEN EVERYTHING SEEMS APART
IN LIFE GOD WILL GIVE HOPE BY
GIVING NEW DESIRE TO PROTECT
SOMEONE OR LOVE SOMEONE
WHICH WE NEVER EXPECTED.

I AM IN A STAGE OF MY LIFE WHERE
I FEEL PEACE WHEN I SURRONDED
MYSELF WITH THE POSITIVE VIBES
AND ONLY ME .

SOMETIMES THE PEOPLE WHO LOVE
US WILL PLAY THE ROLE

OF MAGICIANS .
WHO TRY TO PUT ON A SMILE
ON THE FACE .
WHO TRY TO HEAL
THE BROKEN SOUL .

MAY BE THERE IS A LOT OF
HIDDEN THINGS HIDEN BY
THE HEART .
WHICH WANT TO BURST
IT OUT .
WHICH WANT TO EXPRESS
BUT STILL IT REMAIN QUITE .
BECAUSE SOMEWHERE IT
KNOWS IT WELL PEOPLE
DOESN'T UNDERSTAND EVEN
YOU EXPRESS AND THE REAL ONE
WE DOESN'T NEED TO EXPRESS.

THANKS MY DEAR BEST FRIEND
KARMA .
I HAVE GROWN KIND PERSON
BECAUSE ALWAYS I BELIEVE IN YOU
AND YOU STOOD UP BY MY SIDE.

THE CRAZIEST PEOPLE.
THE KARMA BELIEVERS THEY
DON'T DIRTY THERE HANDS.
EVEN IF YOU HURT THEM BECAUSE
THEY KNOW KARMA HAS A

DELICIOUS MENU FOR YOU .

EVERYTHING COMES AROUND
WHEN YOU ONLY PROVIDE PAIN
TO OTHERS IT WILL SORROW
FLOWERS IN YOUR HOUSE .
NO?
IT SERVE THRONES TO YOU .

BETRAYAL HAS A SPECIAL QUALITY
IT ONLY COMES FROM THOSE
PEOPLE WHOM WE SAID THEY
CAN NEVER HURT US.

I STOPPED SAYING SORRY FOR
THE MISTAKES I HAVENT DONE .
I STOPPED ASKING PEOPLE TO
STAY WITH ME .
I STOPPED ASKING THEM TO
LOVE ME AND I STOPPED CARING
WHEN I FELT I SHOULD STOP
HURTING MYSELF.

SOMETIMES THE BETRAYAL IS IMPORTANT
SO THAT WE CAN UNDERTSND
THE BEAUTY OF PAIN .

ONE DAY WHEN YOU COMPLETELY

HEAL FROM THE PAIN OF BETRAYAL
THEN YOU SURELY UNDERSTAND
WHY LIFE HURTED YOU.
IS TO HEAL YOU.

MAY BE FACES COULD CHANGE
BUT CAN WE ERASE THE
CONNECTION.
WHICH WE FELT WITHOUT
MEETING EACH OTHER.

CAN YOU JUST LISTEN ALL OF MY
CRAZY TALKS ALL OF MY CRAZY TALKS
AND MY MOOD SWINGS WITHOUT
SAYING ANYTHING .
CAN YOU SMILE AT ME AND
SAY THIS WOULD BE FINE ONE DAY ?

WHEN PEOPLE SAY I AM NOT
ENOUGH CAN YOU JUST HOLD
MY HAND AND SAY THAT I AM
THE ONLY ONE YOU HAVE
BEEN LOOKING FOR.

DO NOT GO FOR REVENGE EVERY
PERSON IS DOING THAT .
IF YOU THINK TO DO THEN
WHAT IS THE DIFFERENCE
BETWEEN THEM AND YOU.

YOUR OUTER BEAUTY DOESN'T
DEFINE YOU BUT YOUR
CHARCTER ,YOUR KINDNESS
, YOUR LOVING NATURE.
THE REAL YOU WILL LEAD
TO GENERATE A BEAUTIFUL VIEW.

SOMETIMES ITS OK TO BE
ALONE RATHER THAN WITH
THE PEOPLE WHO CHOOSE
YOU LIKE AN OPTION .

MAY BE EVERY BEAUTIFUL
THINGS COMES UP WITH
A TIME PERIOD .
EVEN IF IT IS PEOPLE
OR BEAUTIFUL MEMORIES .
CHERISH IT WHILE YOU HAVE .

EVERY SMALL THING GETS
ITS VALUE AT A CERTAIN
RIGHT TIME .
THEN YOU ARE HUMAN
DON'T YOU THINK YOU
ARE NOT THAT WORTH
TO GET LOVED?

WHY DO YOU EXPECT
SOMEONE TO LOVE YOU?
WHEN YOU ARE IN PAIN
YOU CRIED BY YOURSELF .
WHEN YOU ARE HAPPY
YOU SMILED.
THEN WHY PEOPLE?

SOMETIMES IT IS HARD
TO SURVIVE.
IN SOME SITUATION BUT
DON'T BLAME THE PROCESS
IT IS LEADING YOU BUILT
A NEW VERSION OF YOURSELF.

WHEN YOU GET VIRUS IN MOBILE
YOU CLEAN IT BUT AT THE SAME
TIME.
THE VIRUS CALLED EMOTIONS ,
NEGATIVE THOUGHTS ,
NEGATIVE PEOPLE WHY DON'T
YOU CLEAN YOUR LIFE .

I TRY MY BEST TO PROTECT SOMEONE
IN MY LIFE BUT IF THE LIMIT
EXCEEDS .
THE ONLY THING I CAN GIFT THEM
IS MY ABSENCE BECAUSE TIME
WILL MAKE YOU UNDERSTAND
WHAT YOU LOST IN YOUR LIFE .

WE ARE LIVING IN A WORLD
WHERE LOYAL PEOPLE ARE
GETTING HATRED AND FAKE
PEOPLE ARE GETTING LOVED .

EVIL SOULS ARE WEARING
THE MASK OF KINDNESS .

I DON'T WRITE FOR ANYONE .
IF SOMEONE THINK I AM POSTING
STUFF FOR PARTICULAR PERSON .
MAY BE I DON'T THINK YOU
DESERVE TO BE IN MY STATUS .

I DON'T LIKE TO BE WITH THE
PEOPLE AND SHARING MY
STUFF AND SAY I CARE
FOR THEM WHEN I DON'T .
I WOULD NOT LIKE THIS
STUFF YOU CALL THIS
ATTITUDE.
I CALL THIS AS THE PRIVATE
PERSON .

CAN WE TRUST SOMEONE AGAIN ?
NO
MAY BE WE CAN TALK BUT

THE BOND AFTER BROKEN IT
COULD NEVER BE THE SAME .

WHEN YOU TRUST GOD THEN
YOU MUST TRUST THAT
THERE IS POWERFULL EVIL
ALSO BECAUSE IN THIS
UNIVERSE EVERYTHING
COMES TOGETHER .

IN THIS WORLD ITS ALL
ABOUT THE APPLICATION
OF YIN AND YANG
HAPPINESS FOR THE DARKNESS ,
PAIN FOR SMILE
TRUST TO BETRAYAL ,
BRIGHTNESS TO DARK .

IN RECENT DAYS MOST HARDEST
THING IS TO TRUST SOMEONE
WITH A NICE WORDS .

NOW A DAYS EVILS ALSO WEARING
A BEAUTIFUL SMILE LOOKING
LIKE AN ANGEL AND DESTROYING
THE SOULS WHEN WE GIVE A
THING THAT CALLED TRUST .

YOU CAN ACHIEVE ANYTHING
IN LIFE IF YOU REALLY
WORK HARD BUT THERE IS
ONLY THING YOU COULDNOT
DO IS TO MAKE SOMEONE
LOVE YOU .
HUMAN EMOTIONS .

SOMETIMES THINK BEFORE
YOU SHARE YOUR HAPPINESS
WITH YOUR TRUSTED ONE
YOU NEVER KNEW.
IF THEY ARE HAPPY
OR DIENG WITH
CUNNINGNESS TO
SEE YOU SMILE .

LOVING SOMEONE IS NOT
A MISTAKE BUT TO LOOSE
YOUR SOUL HAVE THEM
IN LIFE MATTERS
EVERYTHING .

IS IT REALLY REQUIRED TO
HOLD SOMEONE MEMORIES?
WHEN IT IS ONLY GIVING
US HARD TIMES .

THE PERSON WHO ACT COLD

NO ONE CAN LOVE MORE
BEAUTIFUL THEN THE
PERSON WHO SAYS
I DON'T BELIEVE IN LOVE .

BELIVING IN DESTINY
ADDS A HOPE TO
HOPELESS LIFE .

IF SOMETHING IS MEANT
FOR YOU .
NO MATTER HOW HARD
IT IS .
NO MATTER WHO IS
AGAINST YOU .
THE FATE WILL ITSELF
PRESENT IT TO YOU .
WHEN YOU LEAST EXPECT IT .

SOMETIMES WE COULDNOT
FORCE ANYTHING TO
HAPPENING OR NON HAPPENING .
WE JUST NEED TO ACCEPT
THE FLOW OF LIFE .

YOU NEVER NEED TO BE
SORRY FOR BEING YOUR
TRUESELF.

ITS BETTER TO BE ALONE RATHER
THAN HAUNTING PEOPLE
BESIDE US .

WHATS THE MOST SCARRIEST
THING ?
GHOST ?
NO YOUR OWN FEARS
HAVE THAT POWER
TO END YOU .

THERE ARE NOT MANY
PEOPLE WHO WILL
UNDERSTAND YOUR
UNSAID WORDS.

EVERY SMILE HIDES
THE DEEPEST SECRETS .

THE ATTACHEMNENTS WHICH
ARE BROKEN CANNOT BE
FOUND AGAIN .

BELIEVE OR NOT HUMANITY
ERASES ON THE EVERY PHASE
OF LIFE .
PEOPLE FORGET WHAT

UNCONDITIONAL LOVE IS .

WE ARE LIVING IN A
GENERATION WHERE
TRUE LOVE ONLY EXISTS
IN MOVIES AND STORY .
MAY BE IF A PERSON IS COLD .

MAY BE AT A POINT OF
TIME.
I REALIZED .
I AM THE
REASON FOR LETTING
PEOPLE TAKEN GRANTED
OVER ME .

WHEN I SEE BACK
I SMILE BY SEEING
MYSELF HOW CHILDISH
I WAS .

AT A POINT OF TIME
I STOPPED EXPLANING
MYSELF.
I LET IT GO EVERYPERSON .
I CARE FOR AND
SILENTLY WATCHED THEM
GO AND EXPLAINED MYSELF
I WILL BE OK ONE DAY .

I HATED MYSELF FOR
NOT SEEING THE
BEAUTY OF MY SOUL
BEHIND THE SCARS .

THE BIGGEST PROMISE
I DID TO MYSELF NOT TO
TRUST PEOPLE OR ATTACH
WITH THEM AND LESSER
MY VALUE .

MAY BE SOMETIMES THERE
ARE LOT OF WORDS YOU
WANTS TO EXPRESS BUT
YOU COULDNOT BE ABLE
TO EXPRESS BECAUSE ITS
FEEL WORTHLESS.

LIFE IS A GAME OF TIME
AND KARMA .

ENEMIES ARE ALWAYS NOT
OUTSIDERS BUT MOSTLY OUR
NEAR ONCE WHO HOLDS
INVISIBLE KNIFE TO STAB YOU .

MAY BE ITS LOVE OR THINGS
OR RELATIONS .
HOW MUCH WE RUN TO
GET CLOSE THE MORE FAR IT
WILL RUN AWAY FROM YOU .

❧❧❧

SOMETIMES YOU ONLY NEED
TO WORK ON YOURSELF
LEAVE EVERY WORRY ON
DESTINY IT WILL HELP YOU
TO REACH THE THINGS
WHICH YOU LEFT UNSAID .

❧❧❧

WHEN WE UNDERSTAND
WHAT WE NEED IN OUR
LIFE AND WHAT WE WANT IN
OUR LIFE .
MAY BE THE DAY WE REALLY
UNDERSTAND THE MEANING
OF OUR EXISTENCE .

❧❧❧

WHAT DO YOU MEAN BY
HUMANITY ?
ASK YOURSELF ARE YOU
EVEN LOYAL TO YOUR OWNSELF
AND YOUR WHOLE FAMILY .
IF EVERY PERSON STARTS A
LITTLE LOVE WITHIN THEMSELVES
THEY COULD CHANGE WHOLE
NATIONS.

NO ONE CAN UNDERSTAND
YOUR STORY BETTER THEN
YOURSELF SO DONT TRY
TO EXPLAIN EVERYTHING
TO EVERYONE .

IT IS OK IF SOMEONE
HATES YOU .
YOU CANT FORCE SOMEONE
TO LIKE YOU ALL TIME .

REAL MATURITY AND
EDUCATION STARTS
WITH THE PAINFUL
EXPERIENCE IN THE LIFE .

SOMETIMES NOT TO
PEOPLE BUT ATLEAST
WE NEED TO BE LOYAL
TO OUR OWN SOUL .

SOMETIMES WE SHOULD
STOP LYING OURSELVES
THAT WE ARE FINE .

IT IS OK TO BE BROKEN

IT IS OK TO BE EMOTIONAL
IT IS OK TO BE EMOTIONAL
IT IS OK TO GET HURT .
AFTERALL YOU'RE A HUMAN
YOU CANT RUN AWAY FROM
TO HUMAN EXISTENCE .

PAIN IS OUR BESTFRIEND A
SPECIAL GIFT BY THE GOD
BECAUSE OF PAIN WE CAN
SEE THE REAL COLOUR OF
EVERY MASK WEARED BY
THE PEOPLE.

WE ONLY KNOW THE NAME OF
THE PERSON NOT THEIR
STORY TO JUDGE THEM
BEFORE WE KNEW ANYTHING .

SOMETIMES UNIVERSE WILL
REMOVE SOME PEOPLE OR
THING IN LIFE NOT BECAUSE
THEY ARE NOT LOYAL OR
WE NOT LOYAL BUT IT ONLY
REMOVES WHEN WE FORGET
THE REASON FOR OUR EXISTENCE .

WHEN WE FORGET OUR PATH
BECAUSE OF OUR WEAKNESS

OR ADDICTIONS UNIVERSE WILL
REMOVE EVERYTHING FROM US .

SOMETIMES SITTING QUITE EVEN
PEOPLE HURT YOU WHILE WAITING
FOR THE GAME OF KARMA .

SOMETIMES IT IS INTERESTING
TO WATCH KARMA PLAYING
ITS ROLE HEAVENLY .

WHY TO DIRTY YOUR HANDS BY
SEEKING REVENGE EVERYONE
HAS THEIR OWN ACCOUNTS
OF KARMA.

YOU CANT RUN AWAY FROM
THE SITUATIONS OR THE PERSON
FOR THE LONG TIME .
TIME PLAYS CRUCIAL ROLE IT
EVENTUALLY LET YOU FACE
THE THING YOU ALWAYS
WANT TO RUN AWAY FROM.

BEFORE WE HURT A LOYAL
PERSON THINK ABOUT YOUR
OWNSELF.
IF YOU CAN BEAR IF THEY

WILL LEAVE YOU ?
WILL YOU BE ALRIGHT ALL ALONE ?

IF ITS WRITTEN IN YOUR DESTINY .
NO ONE CAN STEAL IT FROM YOU .
IF YOU LOOSE A PERSON OR
THING IN LIFE THEY WERE NEVER
MEANT TO BE YOURS .

YOU CAN ACHIEVE ANYTHING
IN LIFE BUT YOU COULDNOT
CHANGE THE PERSONS
FEELING .

MAGIC EXISTS WITHIN YOURSELF
JUST YOU NEED TO
UNDERSTAND AND FEEL
THE MIRACLES.

Author Pick

LOVE YOURSELF

www.ingramcontent.com/pod-product-compliance
Lightning Source LLC
Chambersburg PA
CBHW022038150726
47990CB00004B/1514